MR. BUMP

by Roger Hargreaves

D0601348

WORLD INTERNATIONAL

This is the sad story of Mr Bump.

The trouble was that Mr Bump just could not help having little accidents.

If there was something for Mr Bump to bump into, he'd bump into it all right.

For instance.

If you were to see Mr Bump out walking down a street in your town, and if there happened to be something to bump into down that street, then you know what would happen, don't you?

BUMP!

Mr Bump was just the same at home.

He lived in an extremely nice home, but even there he couldn't help having those little accidents.

For instance.

One morning when Mr Bump went outside his house he noticed that the chimney pot had come loose in a storm the night before.

"I must fix that before it falls off," thought Mr Bump to himself, and he hurried to his garden shed to fetch a ladder.

It was a very long ladder!

Mr Bump walked up the garden path with the ladder on his shoulder. He turned the corner of the garden path.

CRASH! went the living room window.

"Oh dear," thought Mr Bump, and he turned to see what had happened.

CRASH! went the kitchen window behind him.

"Oh dear," thought Mr Bump again, and he rested the ladder against the wall of the house so that he could climb up on to the roof to mend the chimney pot.

CRASH! went the bedroom window!

So you can see how Mr Bump had his little accidents!

Mr Bump had had many jobs, but somehow they never seemed to last very long.

As soon as anything got lost or broken or splintered or chipped or snapped or cracked or torn or burst or wrenched or crunched or split or slit, Mr Bump got the blame.

For instance.

When Mr Bump worked on a farm, he tripped over the farm dog and spilt the milk which he was carrying for the farmer's wife, and which the farm cat lapped up.

For instance.

When Mr Bump was a postman, he got his hand stuck in a pillar-box, and they had to fetch the fire brigade to come and set him free.

For instance.

When Mr Bump was a bus conductor, he fell off the bus and couldn't catch it up again, and all the passengers travelled without having to pay.

BUS
STOP

For instance.

When Mr Bump was a carpenter, he found that when he was hammering nails he hammered his thumb most of the time and the nail hardly at all.

In order to recover from this series of rather unfortunate happenings, Mr Bump decided to take a holiday. There he could think about what sort of job he could do where he wouldn't be such a nuisance to everybody.

So off he set to the station to catch a train to the seaside.

While Mr Bump was on holiday, several things happened.

For instance.

He fell off a boat into the sea and the lifeboat had to come and rescue him.

For instance.

One day when he was quietly walking along the beach minding his own business he got his foot stuck in a bucket, and as he couldn't get it off he had to walk round with it on his foot for hours.

For instance.

Another time he was walking along the beach, he walked straight into a large hole that somebody had dug, and he had to stay there all night because he couldn't climb out on his own.

However, despite all these little accidents Mr Bump enjoyed his holiday, and while he was there he had a splendid idea about what sort of job he should do.

It was quite the best idea Mr Bump had ever had. An absolutely splendid idea.

And now Mr Bump works happily for Mr Barley the farmer.

Mr Barley has a rather large apple orchard on his farm, and that's where Mr Bump works.

Mr Bump's job is picking apples. But he doesn't use a ladder to climb up the tree to pick the apples like other apple pickers.

Oh no. Mr Bump has a much better way of picking apples than that!

He just walks about!

And before long Mr Bump being Mr Bump walks into a tree.

BUMP!

And down falls an apple. And Mr Bump catches it.

This makes the job of apple picking much easier, and Mr Bump is very pleased about his new job, and Mr Barley is very pleased about his new apple picker.

So you see the story of Mr Bump isn't such a sad story after all. And if you ever bump yourself you know what to do, don't you?

Go and eat an apple picked by Mr Bump, and then you won't feel your bump at all.

You'll remember that the next time you have a bump, won't you?

Good!

MORE SPECIAL OFFERS
FOR MR MEN AND LITTLE MISS READERS

In every Mr Men and Little Miss book like this one, and now in the Mr Men sticker and activity books, you will find a special token. Collect six tokens and we will send you a gift of your choice

Choose either a Mr Men or Little Miss poster, **or** a Mr Men or Little Miss **double sided** full colour bedroom door hanger.

›turn this page **with six tokens per gift required** to:

Marketing Dept., MM / LM, World International Ltd.,
PO Box 7, Manchester, M19 2HD

'our name:______________________ Age: ______

›ddress: ______________________

____

______________________Postcode: ____________

›arent / Guardian Name (Please Print)______________________

›ease tape a 20p coin to your request to cover part post and package cost

enclose six tokens per gift, and 20p please send me:-

›osters:-	Mr Men Poster	☐	Little Miss Poster	☐
›oor Hangers -	Mr Nosey / Muddle	☐	Mr Greedy / Lazy	☐
	Mr Tickle / Grumpy	☐	Mr Slow / Busy	☐
	Mr Messy / Quiet	☐	Mr Perfect / Forgetful	☐
	L Miss Fun / Late	☐	L Miss Helpful / Tidy	☐
	L Miss Busy / Brainy	☐	L Miss Star / Fun	☐

Please Tick Appropriate Box

20p

›tick 20p here please

› may occasionally wish to advise you of other Mr Men gifts.
›ou would rather we didn't please tick this box ☐

100 mm

250 mm

ENTRANCE FEE
3 SAUSAGES

MR. GREEDY

Collect six of these tokens
You will find one inside every Mr Men and Little Miss book which has this special offer.

1
TOKEN

Offer open to residents of UK, Channel Isles and Ireland only

NEW

Full colour Mr Men and Little Miss Library Presentation Cases in durable, wipe clean plastic.

In response to the many thousands of requests for the above, we are delighted to advise that these are now available direct from ourselves,
for only **£4.99** (inc VAT) plus 50p p&p.
The full colour boxes accommodate each complete library. They have an integral carrying handle as well as a neat stay closed fastener.
Please do not send cash in the post. Cheques should be made payable to **World International Ltd. for the sum of £5.49** (inc p&p) per box.

Please note books are not included.

Please return this page with your cheque, stating below which presentation box you would like, t

Mr Men Office, World International
PO Box 7, Manchester, M19 2HD

Your name:____________________________________

Address: ____________________________________

____

________________________Postcode: ______________

Name of Parent/Guardian (please print):________________________

Signature:____________________

I enclose a cheque for £________ made payable to World International Ltd.,

Please send me a Mr Men Presentation Box ☐

Little Miss Presentation Box ☐

(please tick or write in quantity)
and allow 28 days for delivery

Thank you

Offer applies to UK, Eire & Channel Isles only